Peppa Pig™

Fun with Friends

SCHOLASTIC INC.

ISBN 978-0-545-49861-6
Published by arrangement with Entertainment One and Ladybird Books, A Penguin Company.
This book is based on the TV series *Peppa Pig*.
Peppa Pig is created by Neville Astley and Mark Baker.
Peppa Pig © Astley Baker Davies/Entertainment One UK Limited 2003.

12 11 10 9 8 7 6 5 4 3 2 1   13 14 15 16 17 18/0

Printed in Malaysia   106
This edition first Scholastic printing, August 2013

Peppa is playing dress up
with her friend Suzy Sheep.
They are having lots of fun.

Use your stickers to show
Peppa and Suzy playing.

This is Peppa's kitchen. She is helping Mummy Pig make tea.

Use your stickers to decorate Peppa's kitchen.

This is the house where Peppa lives. On sunny days she plays outside with her friends and her little brother, George.

Use your stickers to show Peppa and her friends playing outside.

Peppa and her friends go to playgroup. Their teacher is Madame Gazelle.

Use your stickers to decorate the classroom.

Stickers for pages 2–3

Stickers for pages 4–5

Stickers for pages 6-7

Stickers for pages 8-9

Stickers for pages 10-11

Stickers for pages 12-13

Stickers for pages 14-15

Stickers for page 16

This is Granny and Grandpa Pig's garden. Peppa and George love to help.

Use your stickers to help Granny Pig and Grandpa Pig in the garden.

Peppa and George
sometimes watch TV.
Mummy and Daddy Pig
love to read.

Use your stickers to show
Peppa and her family
spending time together.

On a windy day, everyone loves to fly a kite, especially when there are muddy puddles to play in, too!

Use your stickers to play in the mud with Peppa.

Peppa and George are having a bath. They have to wash off all that mud!

Use your stickers to help Peppa and George get clean.